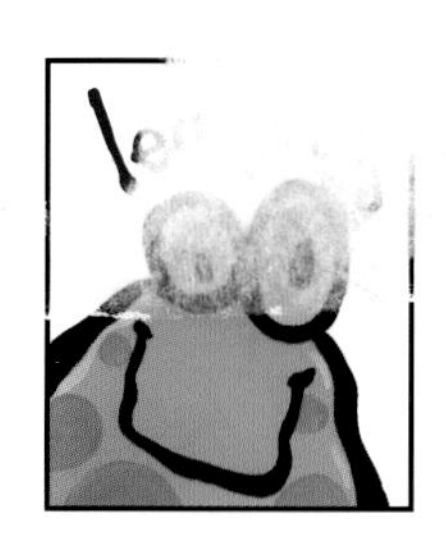

The Little Mermaid

First published in 2006 by
Franklin Watts
338 Euston Road
London
NW1 3BH

Franklin Watts Australia
Hachette Children's Books
Level 17/207 Kent Street
Sydney
NSW 2000

A CIP catalogue record for this book is available from the British Library.

ISBN 0 7496 6577 7 (hbk)
ISBN 0 7496 6583 1 (pbk)

Series Editor: Jackie Hamley
Series Advisor: Dr Barrie Wade
Series Designer: Peter Scoulding

Printed in China

For Katy – my own Little Mermaid – A.A.

The Little Mermaid

Retold by Anne Adeney

Illustrated by Natascia Ugliano

W
FRANKLIN WATTS
LONDON • SYDNEY

Maren was a mermaid princess with a lovely voice.

She lived with her family beneath the sea.

Maren longed to see the world above the surface of the sea, but she was still too young.

On her fifteenth birthday, Maren was allowed to go to the surface like her older sisters.

“It’s so beautiful,”
she thought.

Then Maren saw a ship.
Prince Gustav was having
a party on board.

Suddenly, there was a big storm and the ship quickly sank.

Maren rescued the handsome prince and left him on the beach.

The prince thought another girl had rescued him.
"If only *I* had legs instead of a tail, I could be with the prince," said Maren.

Maren swam home, deep in the sea. She asked Runa, the witch, for a magic potion to give her legs.

Then she would be able to live with the prince above the surface.

"I will give you a potion, but you must pay," Runa warned. "You will lose your voice.

"Your new legs will always hurt you. And if your prince does not marry you, then you will die!"

Maren drank the potion and swam quickly to the surface.

Prince Gustav found her on the beach. She had legs now, but she could not talk or sing.

Maren was taken to
Prince Gustav's palace.

She was so happy, although
her legs hurt her terribly.

Gustav soon fell in love with her. "I love you, but I've promised to marry the girl who rescued me from the shipwreck," he said.

Next day, Gustav got married, but not to Maren.

After the wedding, Maren's sisters came to visit her.

"We gave Runa our hair for a spell to save your life," they said. "If you kill Gustav, you will not die!"

But Maren could

not kill him.

She dived into the sea and melted into the waves.

Then Maren felt herself lifted up into the air.

"We are the spirits of the air," said the magical spirits.

"You have shown great love, so you will never die. And you can live in the sky with us forever!"

Leapfrog has been specially designed to fit the requirements of the National Literacy Strategy. It offers real books for beginning readers by top authors and illustrators.

There are 49 Leapfrog stories to choose from:

The Bossy Cockerel
ISBN 0 7496 3828 1

Bill's Baggy Trousers
ISBN 0 7496 3829 X

Mr Spotty's Potty
ISBN 0 7496 3831 1

Little Joe's Big Race
ISBN 0 7496 3832 X

The Little Star
ISBN 0 7496 3833 8

The Cheeky Monkey
ISBN 0 7496 3830 3

Selfish Sophie
ISBN 0 7496 4385 4

Recycled!
ISBN 0 7496 4388 9

Felix on the Move
ISBN 0 7496 4387 0

Pippa and Poppa
ISBN 0 7496 4386 2

Jack's Party
ISBN 0 7496 4389 7

The Best Snowman
ISBN 0 7496 4390 0

Eight Enormous Elephants
ISBN 0 7496 4634 9

Mary and the Fairy
ISBN 0 7496 4633 0

The Crying Princess
ISBN 0 7496 4632 2

Jasper and Jess
ISBN 0 7496 4081 2

The Lazy Scarecrow
ISBN 0 7496 4082 0

The Naughty Puppy
ISBN 0 7496 4383 8

Freddie's Fears
ISBN 0 7496 4382 X

FAIRY TALES

Cinderella
ISBN 0 7496 4228 9

The Three Little Pigs
ISBN 0 7496 4227 0

Jack and the Beanstalk
ISBN 0 7496 4229 7

The Three Billy Goats Gruff
ISBN 0 7496 4226 2

Goldilocks and the Three Bears
ISBN 0 7496 4225 4

Little Red Riding Hood
ISBN 0 7496 4224 6

Rapunzel
ISBN 0 7496 6159 3

Snow White
ISBN 0 7496 6161 5

The Emperor's New Clothes
ISBN 0 7496 6163 1

The Pied Piper of Hamelin
ISBN 0 7496 6164 X

Hansel and Gretel
ISBN 0 7496 6162 3

The Sleeping Beauty
ISBN 0 7496 6160 7

Rumpelstiltskin
ISBN 0 7496 6165 8

The Ugly Duckling
ISBN 0 7496 6166 6

Puss in Boots
ISBN 0 7496 6167 4

The Frog Prince
ISBN 0 7496 6168 2

The Princess and the Pea
ISBN 0 7496 6169 0

Dick Whittington
ISBN 0 7496 6170 4

The Elves and the Shoemaker
ISBN 0 7496 6575 0*
ISBN 0 7496 6581 5

The Little Match Girl
ISBN 0 7496 6576 9*
ISBN 0 7496 6582 3

The Little Mermaid
ISBN 0 7496 6577 7*
ISBN 0 7496 6583 1

The Little Red Hen
ISBN 0 7496 6578 5*
ISBN 0 7496 6585 8

The Nightingale
ISBN 0 7496 6579 3*
ISBN 0 7496 6586 6

Thumbelina
ISBN 0 7496 6580 7*
ISBN 0 7496 6587 4

RHYME TIME

Squeaky Clean
ISBN 0 7496 6588 2*
ISBN 0 7496 6805 9

Craig's Crocodile
ISBN 0 7496 6589 0*
ISBN 0 7496 6806 7

Felicity Floss: Tooth Fairy
ISBN 0 7496 6590 4*
ISBN 0 7496 6807 5

Captain Cool
ISBN 0 7496 6591 2*
ISBN 0 7496 6808 3

Monster Cake
ISBN 0 7496 6592 0*
ISBN 0 7496 6809 1

The Super Trolley Ride
ISBN 0 7496 6593 9*
ISBN 0 7496 6810 5

* hardback